WHAT THE
WIND BLEW IN

Printed in the United States of America.
To order additional copies of this book, contact:

Writers Branding
1800-608-6550
www.writersbranding.com
orders@writersbranding.com

WHAT THE WIND BLEW IN

6 stories to read with children

written and illustrated by
MARILYN B. WASSMANN

with the assistance of
PAUL A. WASSMANN

Best Wishes
Always from
this author who
spent her childhood
in
Mansfield Center,
Connecticut
1948 —

TABLE OF CONTENTS

Pretend that the WIND blew these by!
Yet know in truth that it was I.
I'm the author and artist capturing tales with lines;
creating couplets and shapes that celebrate rhyme.
Tis a joy to write in verse, I've found.
So please enjoy these words and sounds ...

TIPTOE THROUGH THE TOADSTOOLS

Once upon a time today,
to begin this special rhyme in May.
Under mushrooms, tiny toadstools,
between our willow and oak tree,
an inch high imp just happened to be.

Beneath a sky wearing world-weary gray, while
ambling my meadow-bound way,
on a moment when the sun peaked through,
before clouds came and its smile withdrew. The
winds were spreading the echo of a laugh. A
sunray caught his imp-size shadow slipping past.

Without stirring, though I longed to greet,
I watched the fleeing imp, turned-up nose, spotted feet;
who quickly began to slip backward through a door.
I suppose to his house in the mushroom's core.
For a moment, he sat laughing, waving near the edge;
perhaps fleeing the yellow butterfly who was flying toward the hedge.

I watched closely for the imp's return out of his little round door.
Then looked atop the mushroom, when I heard a snore.
After dining on dewdrop tea and mushroom bread,
he had curved his back to the hump for a snoozable bed.
His tummy rose and fell; his cheeks were red.
Yet he didn't seem too worried about the butterfly he'd fled!

Then suddenly, "Kerplump" and "Ouch!"
A dropping animal object had knocked him from his couch.
The imp looked above and glared--
And "What are you to dare … ?"
"I beg your pardon, ask 'Who, not what'?"
the animal replied from the bottom of a rut.
"I'm just as much a someone … a dragonfly!"
the animal said. "Oh no, but this is my home, my land, my, my…"
the interrupting, impolite imp cried.

"Pardon me," said the animal on top of the mushroom tree,
"but I regret to interrupt you as you've done to me.
I was trying to tell you that I'd hurry on my way.
But I would rather make a friend than foe … before I go…
What's your name? I'm Flonster the Dragonfly … I…"
Yet before he finished, he fell down below.
For that naughty imp shook the stalk with a five toe blow!
Then he climbed back on top, crying "Yip-yip-dee-do!"

"Ouch!" cried the dragonfly, who now stared above,
at an imp he felt certain had never learned to love.
"Please listen, please try.
I saw you tease that butterfly,
by sticking honey on its wings;
must be like your other impish flings …!"
"Perhaps you don't remember your name

because there aren't any friends to call you to games."
Suddenly the imp cried: "Did you say you were a dragonfly?
Oh my, I should have let you be!
My grandma said dragons would blow fire on me!"

With that, the imp disappeared in a hole in the mushroom top,
banged his feet down the staircase within,
and poked his head out with a pop!
"Don't blow fire at me for what I've done.
I know I'm an imp without any friend or anyone.
There are not any other 'me's' said my grandma
who lives on lichens, the ladybugs, and bees.
Not another imply mushroom eater like me,
between the pond, the willow, and the oak tree."
"Ha, ha!" laughed the dragonfly, "then like me, you're extraspecial too—
then why would I breathe fire on you?"

"Only maiden-stealing dragons have fire for fantasy princes,
in realms of never-land above.
And if you had really been listening,
and for everyone felt a little more love,
you'd have noticed that in falling twice,
I've really bent my wing.
And I wish you wouldn't be unfriendly,
but try to do something.
I was so lucky to fall first on your soft mushroom top.
Yet I didn't expect to fall on harder ground, plip-plop!"

After listening this time, the imp looked differently at the dragonfly.
Then quivered, looked down, and made a humble cry.
For he knew that he wanted to feel and show more than teasing, selfish ways, and
let his inner, thoughtful warmth shine for others today.
So smiling softly, he said, "Hello dragonfly, I'm Momanderly Beselflen, You
said Flonster was your name. I'm so happy now to know you…
Let me think if I can help you with that lame – So sorry that it happened to you!
Ah-ha, two pieces of mushroom just might do!"
Then bouncing out, he collected the pieces and a string of grass.

He pulled the bent wing quickly up and fastened it in cast.
"Now you have to stay still for a day or so.
And you're welcome to stay here you know."
"Thank you," said Flonster, with a dragonfly grin.
"Let's watch the sun going to bed before we go within."
"We've a lot to share and care you'll see."
Then the imp agreed and laughed with new glee—
"Oh, I think the world should be full of special friends like you and me.
Oh, it's extra-extra special that we happened to be!"

A raindrop fell sprinkling the two "ping-in-in-in."
A rainbow found its end and swung high above,
as they giggled and scampered to a warm within.
Watching quietly, I felt raindrops "plip-plop," touching me from above.
I too sought home, yet changed, much more aware of the wonder of love.

BALLAD OF THE BIRDHOUSE

Imagine a hole in a birdhouse wall,
and three birds who were tiny and just so small.
Picture one chirping with his beak opened wide,
calling to his mother who was not inside.

Of course, she was returning, but he just couldn't rest,
Not while his mother was away from HIS nest.

Well, he tried to awaken his brothers with his bill.
But they just didn't move, they were so still,
sleeping and dreaming about their next meal,
knowing how warm their mother would feel--

When she settled again in their home hanging high,
on a pole in our yard, beneath our blue sky.

Yet on that morning in the month of May,
the bird's mother was busy and far away;
looking for nourishment for her baby birds' tongues,
like insects and beetles to feed her young.

She was just hoping that her birds would only lie,
in their nest waiting for her until they could fly.

But one baby bird moved away from the rest,
and looked out of the hole at the edge of his nest.
He saw a plastic owl perched on a branch nearby.
Then he looked out into our yard and up to the sky.

"So where are you going when you're mother's not here?"
asked the owl who knew no one else was near.

"You simply don't realize how really high you are.
The lawn in this backyard is just so far,
below your safe and secure nest with your brothers nearby.
Or are your wings strong and you're ready to FLY?"

"And besides your mother flew away on a breeze,
to search for bugs, maybe moths, that she could seize."

Well, the baby bird shuttered after the speech of the owl.
He felt very confused, yet he tried not to scowl.
He had heard his mother say those words "to fly."
Yet he hadn't been listening when she told her birds why.

Oh why, oh why, was he dreaming when she
told them how she moved from tree to tree.

Then the young bird said "I am restless in this nest!
And just what would happen if I left the rest
of these birds who will probably sleep till they've grown,
while I simply long for adventures of my own."

When the owl had heard this tiny bird,
he paused to carefully choose his words:

"You're still not listening, especially to the sounds,
of danger and troubles that are all around.
Maybe you're ready, but your wings look small to me.
And when you can't fly, you'll fall, you'll see!"

Now this baby bird was trying to understand what he'd been told.
But he needed to find his mother, and I guess that he was bold.

Perhaps he was thinking that he would know how to fly, when
he left their home which was hanging high--

On a pole in our yard, where he decided that he would
be able to fly with a one, two, three …

Instead, he spun, he rolled, he fell.
His fall was worse than I can tell.

Unfortunately, the bird had not been taught to sing.
He didn't even know that he could flap his wing,
which might have helped him rise in the air,
stay aloft, and maybe even travel somewhere.

As the bird fell, he was frightened, he shrieked, and started to cry.
But that bird, poor bird, he just could not FLY!

Now maybe it's not possible, yet when people aren't around,
imagine inanimate objects magically moving without a sound.
Especially when there's a need to correct a tragic mistake,
and that's why the bird was rescued for the plastic owl was AWAKE!

So just be happy for that lucky bird landing on our soft flower bed.
He was winded, shaken, ruffled, but he wasn't really dead!

Besides, the owl was listening, and he heard the baby bird moan,
"Oh why, oh why, am I now so alone?
Oh mother, mother, I'm in trouble now,
and maybe if I'd been listening, I might know how--

To fly, not fall, out of our nest,
I just should have waited like the rest!"

Well, owls in the wild can swoop down on their prey.
They grab them with their claws and carry them away,
for food, I'm sure, but plastic owls don't eat!
And our owl, wise owl, he was just so sweet!

Sweet, because he swooped down for the bird;
aware of his plight and glad the he'd heard:

The bird admitting to his tragic choice,
crying for his mother with his little voice.
His limbs were hurting from his sudden fall,
but the plastic owl could lift him because he was small.

"You were lucky just this time, my restless little friend!
But remember, with one careless move, in a second, life can END!"

The owl hooted these words, and returned the bird to the birdhouse on the pole.
And with these lines, I think, this story is almost told.
However, I must add that the mother saw the rescue of her bird.
And as she was flying home, she must have heard--

The owl offering his very helpful advice.
And surely that mother bird didn't have to think twice.

So before he froze again on his perch, she flew down to thank that owl,
to say she completely agreed with the message that he had howled,
to her wayward son, who was oh, so lucky on that day.
She was quite upset, and she scolded him right away!

Then the mother bird fed her group with the moth that she had found
in the distance, near our pond, and close to the ground.

"We're moving my sons, and you simply must learn,
to FLY!," she said, and her voice was stern.
"Like one of you did today, you'll fall from this spot."
Then the baby bird added "It can be so disastrous if you
should be listening and you're not!"

Now the baby bird was really a little like you and me.
He'd fallen, he'd been rescued, and he had really learned to see:

That it's really better to learn a skill,
listen, study, practice, and then you will
remember to be careful with every step that you take,
and you'll be safe not sorry for the choices you make.

And then, well, maybe, not quite like that bird, but
probably just as HIGH!
Yes, you'll try, and then like that baby bird, you will
FLY!!

TALE OF A TIGGER

Oh, wouldn't it be nice to have time to chat,
with people and children and even your cat.
Cleaning and cooking wouldn't get in our way.
Imagine our talking throughout the day.

After all, we're alive, and observing it all.
Of course, I should tell you, I am rather small.
And I'll be honest at once and spare you illusions.
I'm a creature that's not very fond of confusion.

Therefore, I'll clarify my position, so we can move on from there.
You see, I'm only a cat, but pull up your chair.

Well, life can be lonely, but I know I'm not bitter.
Still, I'll confess that I do miss my litter.
My brothers, my sisters, my mother; they're gone;
living in my memories, yet they're yesterday's song.

I'd summarize my beginnings, yet there's more in details.
Besides most cats are clever and spin amazing tales.
Tales which are stories, yet cats also have a "tail."
We wave them so proudly like a boat in full sail.

I remember discovering mine when I was just a kitten.
I was fascinated by it then, and I'm still quite smitten …

With that appendage that let's you know I'm a cat.
And then there's my eyes, my ears, but there's more than that.
As a cat, I move in a quick, smooth, and purposeful way.
I am so independent, yet I do love to play.

I'm sure my father wasn't aware of my family or me.
He was just a large tomcat, so wild and so free.
Moving around from yard to yard and town to town,
He simply couldn't imagine "settling down."

Even with my mother, that sweet enticing feline.
He wooed her from a distance, and waited for a sign-

Of interest, of course, but she was so coy,
domesticated and proud, afraid to enjoy
the company of other cats that passed by her door,
until she met my dad who radiated with "something more."

More than appeal, my dad was a charmer.
Mother never dreamed that he would harm her.
But their quick affair led to my brothers, my sisters, and me.
Isn't it quite special how we're each born to be?

So now, each day, I try to celebrate that,
I was born to be a CAT!!!

And now that I'm a cat, not a kitten, I value my name of "TIGGER!"
I'm ferocious, lots of trouble, yet I am so very eager
to tell you a little about what it feels like to be in my place, to be alive,
energetic, yet limited by my space.

When you are a kitten, everything is imposing and tall.
Now, I'm a cat, and this house seems small.
Small, because I've explored each corner, window, and door.
I long to explore beyond this for I know there's more …

More spaces, more people, more animals and yet,
it's just so risky and I'd probably not let--

My body travel beyond this place, for there's really no place like home.
No doubt I'd find trouble if I let myself roam.
Besides life is quite comfortable, I'm fed twice a day.
My master is retired, and my mistress works away--

From this house, in which four dogs also live.
They're small, aging creatures, but I always give
them plenty of space when they decide to pass me.
They sleep quite often, and one really can't see.

Cataracts bother Fuji, along with the tangle in his fur.
He stays close to his master who he must see as a blur.

There's a nice, warm body to sleep with on the floor.
Her name is Tomo, and she's the female in this group of four.
And Perry is so passive like a black and white stuffed bear.
I often wonder if he's ever really aware--

Of Rabbit, the fourth dog who steals all of their snacks.
He was born one Easter, and he rarely lacks
energy; so he often barks to send me into a different space.
Because like the others; he's uneasy when I'm near his face.

You see, all of these dogs have very large eyes.
To scratch them with my claws would be extremely unwise.

Why anger my master for he's not that fond of me.
When he screams "CAT," then watch me flee!
Quite often I jump to the floor, and hide under a chair.
For the times when I please him are really quite rare.

In contrast, I purr when my mistress is around.
She's always glad to see me, and I know she likes the
sound of my purring and my occasional "meouwing" call.
She feeds me, I'm fond of her, and well, that's all.

Of course, I do treasure several windows inside,
and the spots where I can play or simply hide.

In this house in which I travel around,
most of the time I move without a sound.
Objects I pass brush against my fur.
Yet my masters would be angry so I rarely stir--

Anything, yet some places puzzle me, although you might understand.
One is on top of the bedroom's bureau to the right of the light stand.
It's like the windows in some of the other spaces.
Yet it seems to open up in a room like I'm in, with identical places.

Everything's in reverse, and there's a cat that looks exactly like me.
I've tried to get his attention, but mostly I just let him be.

He seems to be exploring his house just like I always do.
But he ignores my presence, and I haven't any reason or clue.
Why he rarely notices me, or why he doesn't want to play.
Or whether he would be able to enter my space in some way.

I saw him in another room high on a bedroom wall.
Yet not for long on that bookcase, because I was afraid I'd fall.
Again he looked like me, but he seemed in a hurry to depart.
I wanted to make him my friend, but how would I be able to start--

Meowing to him when he moved away into his space.
Why didn't he want to come to play or maybe even race?

He remained a mystery, yet it was nice to know he was there.
I often sat on my master's bureau and took some time to stare.
The land behind that window seemed so real, yet it remained to be seen
if I joined that cat, would he be friendly or very, very mean?
I really needed that cat's help one afternoon.
Although I knew that my mistress would be coming home soon,
my master was preparing dinner by cooking a meatloaf with cloves.
And everything was getting so hot in the oven and on the stove.

Yet my master seemed so tired, and he'd gone to take a nap.
The pups were curled up near him, and one leaned against his lap.

The smoke detector was broken, so I tried to rouse them with my "meowing" call.
But unfortunately that didn't really disturb them at all.
I scampered to the mysterious window for the help of that cat.
But he just wouldn't move from where he sat.

Looking at me in a very nervous way.
I felt exactly like him, and it occurred to me that day.
That the cat on the wall was really just me.
Somehow that window reversed images and you could see--

Something I later learned was a mirror, a reflection.
A large picture of everything in my direction.

Not another world beyond that wall.
Just the space I was in, and well, that's all.
So that cat couldn't help, and I needed a noise.
So I ran into another room, and searched among my toys.

Animals stuffed with catnip were of little use to me now.
I began to think that I just didn't know how,
to make any noise without knocking a shelf down.
But then I really began to look all around.

And in a corner of that very room,
wasn't it quite fortunate that I noticed a BALLOON …

A bright, red balloon that my mistress had collected;
dangling above me and looking quite neglected.
Well, I do need to reach the end of this rhyme.
And the clock was ticking; there wasn't really time.

Besides that balloon was quivering; it probably did not want to break.
And yet how else would I be able to wake
my master and the pups who were snoring on the couch.
So my claws came out, hit the balloon, and I heard an "OUCH!

Or maybe it was just the air exploding from the balloon's inside.
But the noise was quite loud, and the balloon collapsed on its side.

And that noise, it was a welcome sound disturbing my family's ears.
That popping balloon, it awoke them all, and took away most of my fears.
And really I can't remember seeing anyone move faster
than the time that stove was discovered by my master!

My master screamed, turned off the oven, and I waited for him to see.
He remembered waking to a popping sound, and he noticed the balloon beside me.
He realized that I had wanted to alert him to the danger in our home.
He seemed quite amazed that I had searched and found a solution of my own.

I know now that it was their respect that I had won
when my master told my mistress about what I had done.

My mistress had arrived after a long work day.
She listened to my master who had so much to say
about the way that I had heroically roused him from his sleep,
with a balloon that I had broken with just one very purposeful leap!

My mistress rewarded me with a dinner of tasty meats.
My master seems more generous, and he often gives me treats.
He fixed the smoke detector; he naps with an alarm clock now.
I'm a proud cat concluding this story by taking a final bow.

Because when my owners sent this tale to the newspaper in our town,
the headline announced that "A CAT HAD KEPT A HOUSE FROM BURNING DOWN!"

WHY CRY BUTTERFLY?

Why cry Butterfly?
We need to know so we could try,
to cheer you up so you could fly.
Why do you cry Butterfly?

Why cry in the lovely month of May?
Did you wound your wing in the yard today?
Did you find that you were flying the wrong way?
Or perhaps you stopped because you wanted to say,
something to your friends who had gathered to play?
Just why are you crying anyway?

Perhaps they ran into you as you were flying past?
You've bent your wing; maybe you need a cast?
Would that we could help to heal you fast.
Your time being disabled just can't last ...

That long, because there's so much to do.
Time marches on even when you're blue.
We really wish that we could help you.
Watching you fly makes us happy too!

Maybe you were hurt when a flower or petal closed?
Or were you caught as you moved away to avoid those
flowers that bend and sway as they grow,
or the leaves that flutter when the wind blows?

Into the path of a bird passing by?
Did that happen when you flew too high?
Oh butterfly, you really adorn our sky,
and we look for answers and wonder why ...
Why you should be so wounded and still?
We'll keep you safe and warm until
you'll fly again; you wait and see.
Moving around is the way you should be!

Maybe your tears will ease your pain.
Experiences of our lives do often strain
our bodies, our feelings, our hearts, our brains.
It's time to slow down; maybe even watch the rain.

Why cry Butterfly? With time, you'll probably mend.
Besides, look at that animal; he's just arrived. Could he be your friend?
He looks like you, but his wings are flapping to show concern.
Maybe from him, we'll be able to learn
why you can only flutter and crawl.
Did you collide with a window or wall?
Just what was the cause of your tragic fall?

Because something did happen, and your friend's so distressed.
Can't he see now that you just need some rest?
He's waiting so patiently; he wants you to fly.
Maybe you're not that injured, and you ought to just try.

When bad things happen, sometimes we'll never know why.
All we can do is weep and then cry.
And hope that someday, we will start to fly high.
Again, just like you, Sweet Butterfly!

We noticed that you're suddenly stronger today.
Your friend is waiting, and we wanted to say:
Get ready, feel healthy, and just fly away!

We did enjoy looking at your colorful wings;
the lines that decorate them, and yes, those rings,
that moved whenever you fluttered or stirred.
You were a lovely sight, *oh* yes, you were!

But now, time has passed, and you have been stirring.
Like your friend, your wings are definitely whirling.
Your wounds have healed; they weren't that bad.
You'll be able to fly, and we are so glad.

Why cry anymore, Sweet Butterfly? Wounds can heal!
And now, let's just celebrate because we feel
relieved to know that you're finally O.K.
We saw you flying around our yard today.
From flower to flower in our garden in the sun,
with time to enjoy life and to just have fun!!!

FLUBE-A-DUBE

I hurry, I'm tired, I want to be home.
My mind is on problems that are more than my own.
So returning from work, I tend to ignore
"Flube-a-,Dube" greeting me at the door.

He's not one of the pets who move about inside.
He depends on our dog "Duchess" to give him a ride,
around the house, but most often to the door.
He's there, this toy animal, inside, on the floor.

His colors are clashing, they're vivid, they scream.
He's a mixture of yellow, magenta, and green.
White buttons on his face have become his eyes.
Four legs on his body have increased his size.

Now "Flube" as we call him when there so little time,
deserves this story, this tale, this rhyme.
We can't see his bruises, but there's bound to be some.
He is dragged all around, and he's probably quite numb.

He is pulled by a foot, a tail, an ear,
from room to room, over there or here.
He knows what to expect each and every day.
He's the favored toy when the pups start to play.

His stare is fixed permanently, and he can't even blink,
yet "Flube-A-Dube" is really a soldier in spirit I think.
If he could cry out, perhaps he would howl.
But no, he just seems more like an owl.

Yes, like an owl who stares while he is still.
You don't really see them doing anything until
something quite significant happens near their space;
their feathers become ruffled and out of place.

Flube is not an owl, yet he has a lot to observe in our home.
And he's on the floor in a room where he's rarely alone.
He's in a small breakfast room with books and newspapers all around,
and the place is also filled with cages and the birds' chirping sounds.

Now, Flube is sometimes swept under the table by my ever-active broom.
And he'is often left upside down when he's transported around the room.
When this occurs, it seems to me, Flube takes the most logical leap.
He sinks into himself, and then he falls into a deep, deep, deep, deep sleep.

Unfortunately, this happens quite often so Flube's really rested.
How lucky it is that he is rarely tested!
He does survive the ritual of being a gift at our front door.
And he patiently endures when Duchess decides to shake him on the floor.

"Flube-A-Dube" spends so much time under the table.
And at first, we believed that he was really rarely able,
to move without our help or the action of our dogs.
It's sad that he'll never walk, or run, or even jog.

Poor Flube, you say, and you are probably right,
but even he became a hero the other night.
You see, he watches the pets who are living with him,
the pups, the fish, the birds on limbs.

He was closest to a cockatiel he could see from below,
and a lovebird across the room that he started to know
When one pup grabbed him, and he should have said "Ouch!"
Because the pup pulled him up, and left him on the couch.

Our lovebird has eyes encircled by black feathers, and her body is turquoise blue.
And when she saw Flube, she chirped away to let him know all that she knew
about the man of the house, his working wife, their pets, and so much more.
According to her, most of the birds in the room definitely feared an open door.

Now, I really must return to the night when Flube amazed us so.
Apparently, he just fell off of the couch as far as we know.
Yet it happened at such an incredibly appropriate time
that I simply must describe the situation in this rhyme.

Well, from the floor, Flube had been watching the cockatiel now and then.
Although he couldn't talk to them, he regarded the birds as his friends.
Perhaps proximity binds creatures especially when a crisis occurs,
and Flube happened to be up on the couch when he saw the cockatiel stir.

Our cockatiel moved toward the cage door that was abnormally ajar.
This frightened Flube who knew that the bird should not go very far
beyond his space because the other animals would grasp his wings.
And that would be the end of this bird who could really, really sing!

And of course, it was near supper time, and the cats and pups were hungry too.
They were probably hoping that the flavors of food were finally something new.
They hovered about as I worked to fill their dishes and collect what we would eat,
and in all that commotion, who would have heard the cockatiel begin to tweet?

Tweet because he was frightened, but he was also tempted to fly.
Even Flube could understand that most birds long to see the sky.
But in that room, the bird's flight would be brief; he'd hit a window or the ceiling.
And to any creature, the sight of an injured animal is never very appealing.

Therefore, just when the bird was hovering near the ledge.
That's when Flube must have decided to fall off the edge
of the couch, and his fall distracted a dog who was watching nearby.
It also alerted my husband who suddenly understood why.

Something was wrong, and luckily he was looking near the cage of the bird!
He wondered how long it had been open, and he was glad that he had heard
the louder cries of the other birds, and he noticed Flube in the middle of the floor.
Perhaps, it might have been a perfect time for my husband to rant and roar!
However, everyone was lucky when he closed the door quite quickly.
Avoiding a situation which could have been very, very prickly!

Now I know it's hard to believe that any stuffed animal could move or feel.
But maybe that day, Flube felt something and he rescued our cockatiel!
In any case, it's exciting when we decide to travel or roam.
But, yes, it's best for all of us when we simply choose to stay home.

MICE WORKS

The cheese was so tempting: the mice needed a slice.
But after sampling it on the shelf, they had to think twice .
Was the cat on the shelf above porcelain or real?
The mice hurried away before his next meal.

Now these mice were very lucky to be so small.
They scurried away through some cracks in the wall.
Together, they carried a piece of the cheese;
a night time snack they chose to seize.

But one mouse got stuck in the crack; he'd made a dreadful choice.
He was just a little too wide and he cried out in a squeaky voice.
And if the cat on the shelf was real, he probably would not be blind.
He'd see that that mouse had definitely left his rear section behind.

Poor mouse, you say, and we totally agree,
His cry reached his friends who were able to see
his dangerous predicament, his vulnerability.
Imagine if such a thing happened to you or to me?

What would you do to escape the cat's claws?
Be spared his attack and even his jaws?
Think thin, perhaps, and pull yourself through!
Was this something our poor mouse could do?

Alas it's sad but every creature reaches a certain size,
and our mouse's eating habits had not been wise.
Food warmed him so from his head to his feet,
and that is why he really loved to EAT!

Now in a snowstorm, we wait for the sun, a shoveler, or a plow.
Surely other people will come to rescue us some way, somehow.
And clearly our mouse was trapped so he needed to depend
on the fact that he was really missed by his friends.

Fortunately, this mouse just happened to be more than a steady eater.
He was in fact the group's most treasured leader.
And he was urgently moving his tail from side to side,
hoping the crack would become a little more wide.

Besides the cat or the shelf had started to stir.
What might have been porcelain was in reality cat's fur.
The cat was looking for a way to jump down from the shelf;
a path to the floor without hurting himself.

Meanwhile, the mouse's movements changed the shape of the shelf's wall.
And luckily the mouse's friends had heard his urgent call.
Several mice returned and started to chew away some of the wood.
The group struggled to free him if they could.

So even without their trusted leader, the mice began to work together!
Some scurried toward a nearby shelf with balls of wool and yes, a feather.
They recognized that these objects would distract,
hopefully keep the cat busy, and also attract
him away from the mice trying to rescue their friend.
Their chewing was steadily freeing his tail end.

Now mice are often caught by cats, but yes, they can get ahead.
Especially, if they work together and somehow use their heads!
As a group, some of these mice moved the feather and made the ball of wool
fall off the nearby shelf by jointly struggling to push and pull.

And so these objects fell, and the cat on the shelf decided to pounce!
The mice's actions made the feather and the ball of wool bounce.
The cat did see the mice but he simply could not ignore
the feather and the ball of wool moving along the floor.
He was drawn to the movement and he really longed to chase
the moving objects to pull and push around his space.

Yet as he chased these moving shapes, he also saw the mice.
If he caught any one of them, one blow from his claws would suffice
to end their lives, so before the cat turned completely around,
the mice came together on the shelf and quickly scurried down.
And none of the mice wanted to be the last
They hurried, they fled, they moved so fast!

They ran back to the shelf with their friends who had started moving away.
They did not want to be food for the cat; they couldn't afford to stay.
And by the time the cat turned from chasing the wool to pursue the fleeing mice,
the empty shelf he saw was bad for him, but for the mice, quite nice!
They had all escaped his potentially dangerous claws.
They were also spared from being food for his very lethal jaws!

The cat rarely returns to the top of the shelf anymore.
It's just too high, and he's busy with objects moving around the floor.
The chubby mouse is thinner; he chooses cracks that he can move through with ease!
And all of the mice are careful when they come for a slice of cheese!!